Illustrations | Photoshop
Layout | Indesign

Some design elements were downloaded from Pixabay.com

ISBN-13: 978-1-7330872-3-0

Oh dear Santa, it's almost the end of the year,
and I wish Christmas morning was already here!

We have hung all our lights, and ol' Frosty's all done,
and the whole house OUTSIDE is deliciously fun!

But, dear Santa, there's something I've just got to say:
there've been strange goings-on IN my house here today.

To be honest, I've noticed it almost all week.
And it's thoroughly odd, and it's terribly bleak.

See; the cookies are gone, and the eggnog is out,
and there's green Christmas wrappings all lying about.

There is NO cocoa left, only white empty mugs,
and of course, all the crumbs on my Mom's persian rugs.

And some presents are missing, and the cider is too!
Where the red ribbons went to, I haven't a clue!

And the last time I saw all the caramel bars,
was when Mom put them next to the candy cane jars.

And I know it's not big Uncle Clyde and Aunt May,
'cause they won't come for supper until Christmas Day!

And my Grandma and Grandpa are ever so cool;
they will NOT break the

RED, GREEN AND WHITE
CHRISTMAS RULE!

NEVER

open the presents,

DO NOT

eat all the cake.

WAIT

until Christmas morning;

DO IT, FOR GOODNESS' SAKE!

I have even asked Dad, but he just shook his head,
and went shoveling the snow in our driveway instead.

Even Sox turned her head and my dog wagged his tail
when I showed them the pretzel and chocolaty trail.

When I asked my three friends, Dominique, Luke and Tommy, they just said: "Watch out, man; it's the great

CHRISTMAS MOMMY!

With a sweet tooth, she's sly and she comes in the night,
and she tries all your food and she takes a big bite

of the puddings and pastries and all she can eat.
Then she leaves with a present and a peppermint treat."

It has nothing to do with who's naughty or nice,
even IF there's a list that you have to check twice!

And my friends said there's no house that's safe on the block,
'cause the sly Christmas Mommy does NOT have to knock.

She has ribbons and bows in her green and white hair,
and her parachute glows when it opens midair.

And her pink rosy cheeks lighten up while she giggles,
as she melts all the snow when she jumps, squats and wiggles.

Even though she knows Santa, whom she sees once a year,
this particular mommy isn't even from here!

She is fond of the North, but the South Pole is home,
where she lives with her penguins Bouffant and Jerome.

And Cilantro and Daubert and Puddles and Sven
help her take to the skies every now and again.

So how DOES she slide RIGHT DOWN our long chimney fluke?
There's no hole big enough; I made sure when I looked.

And our windows are shut; there's no footprints outside.
And there's practically no space inside here to hide.

And, Dear Santa, I'm worried, 'cause my Mom isn't well.
She has heard of this very strange tale, I can tell.

'Cause she cries every time she goes back to the store,
and then comes home to find that she needs to buy more

of the presents and candies that we all cannot find.
It's a terrible, horrible weight on her mind!

So I'm wondering, dear Santa, since it's getting quite late, could you send Mrs. Claus to my house, number Eight,

to help batter and bake all the treats that are gone?
I'll make sure that my Dad leaves the kitchen light on.

And then please send the elves to help finish the tree
and the stockings and bows. I am sure you'll agree

it will make my Mom smile like my Dad's ugly sweater.
And my Dad will be glad that it made her life better.

So dear Santa, the front key is under the rug.
And please DO give ol' Rudolph a very big hug!

For more adventures, visit

www.ingridsawubona.com

For Snoopy

Made in the USA
Coppell, TX
12 December 2020

44283628R00029